Kumo

the
bashful
cloud

WRITTEN BY Kyo Maclear

ILLUSTRATED BY Nathalie Dion

tundra

If you look at the edge of the big blue sky . . .

you might see Kumo.

For many years, her only wish was to float unseen.

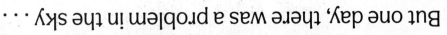

But one day, there was a problem in the sky . . .

Cumulus was under the weather.

Cirrus had traveled to a cloud convention.

Kumo was called for cloud duty — to shade and
shower those below.

"Oh no," said Kumo. "I can't possibly
go out there alone."

Her hopes of remaining soft and invisible evaporated.

Kumo pulled all her fluff together and
began to wobble slowly across the sky.

Her mind was heavy with doubt.
What if people point?
What if I'm too airy?
Too stormy?
Too wispy?

She squeezed her eyes shut.

What a mistake.
She was stuck.

Fortunately, a friendly kite

came along to help.

And a kindly wind gave an extra lift.

It felt good to be free again.

Kumo drifted over noisy cities
where buildings shifted the shape of the sky

and crossed a warm lake, lapping water as she went.

She lingered over rolling fields
where she released a few tears of rain

and skimmed the singing glaciers,

briefly touching the ice.

She offered a man shelter as he planted

petunias in a pretty row . . .

And came upon a large
street party where people in colorful
clothes were putting on a show.

A few children pointed at Kumo,
but she didn't notice.

Kumo had found a small boy
with his head in the clouds.

And sometimes dreaming helped.

Kumo knew it was hard being small in such a big place.

It's good to be a cloud who is seen, she thought.

A traveling cloud with a job to do
and a whole world to visit.

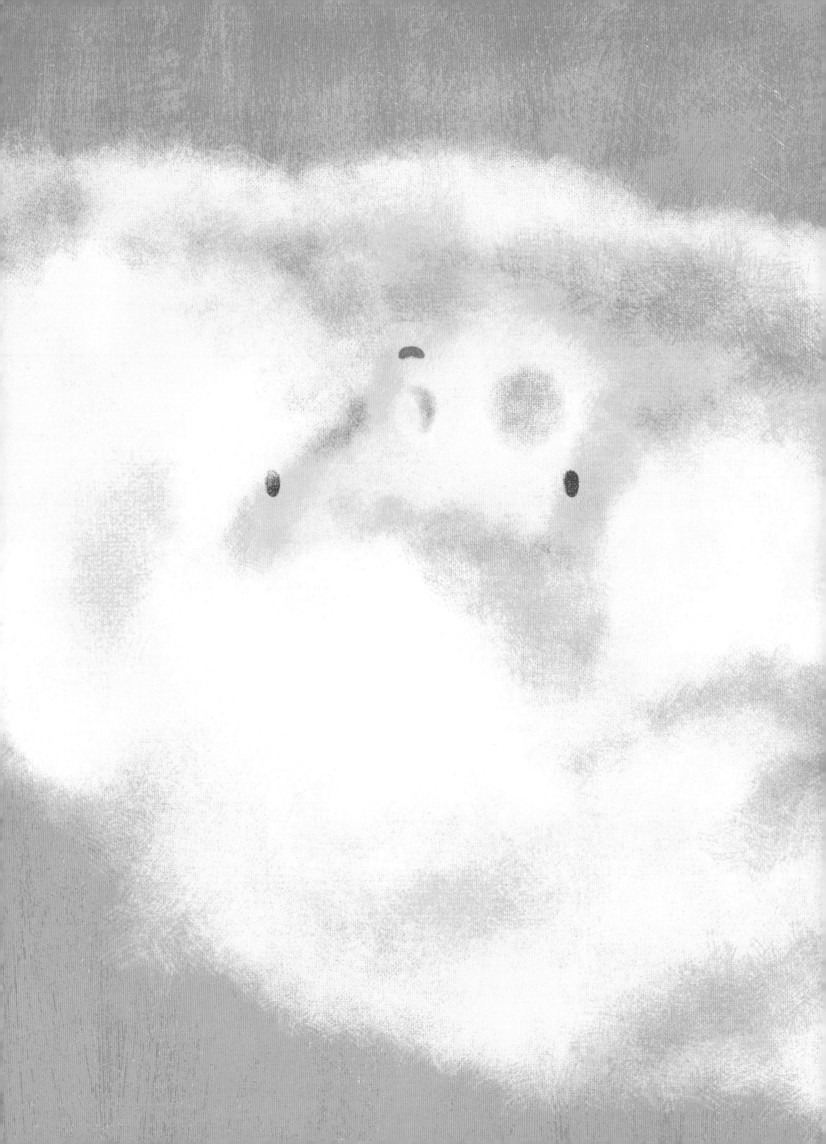

It's good to be a cloud who is unseen,

when everything is quiet.

When there are mountains to slip behind,
once, twice, for a little rest.

Sailing to the top of the world, she came upon
a few clouds she had never seen before.

Kumo drew in a deep breath and inched toward them,

wondering if such big, beautiful clouds could

ever want her company . . .

They did!

Her new friends were named
Fuwa-chan, Miruku and Mochi.
Together they streamed across the sky,
collecting other clouds along the way . . .

Until there were clouds and clouds and clouds
everywhere, joining together,
becoming the whole sky.

For a moment, Kumo forgot all about herself.

What peace, what friends, what . . .

What happened?

The sky darkened.

The air stilled.

Clouds scattered as the
ground cooled.

Kumo had just grown used to being part of a group

when she found herself alone again.

But not completely alone . . .

"Look," said Kumo.

Mochi drifted toward her.

"Look," said Kumo.

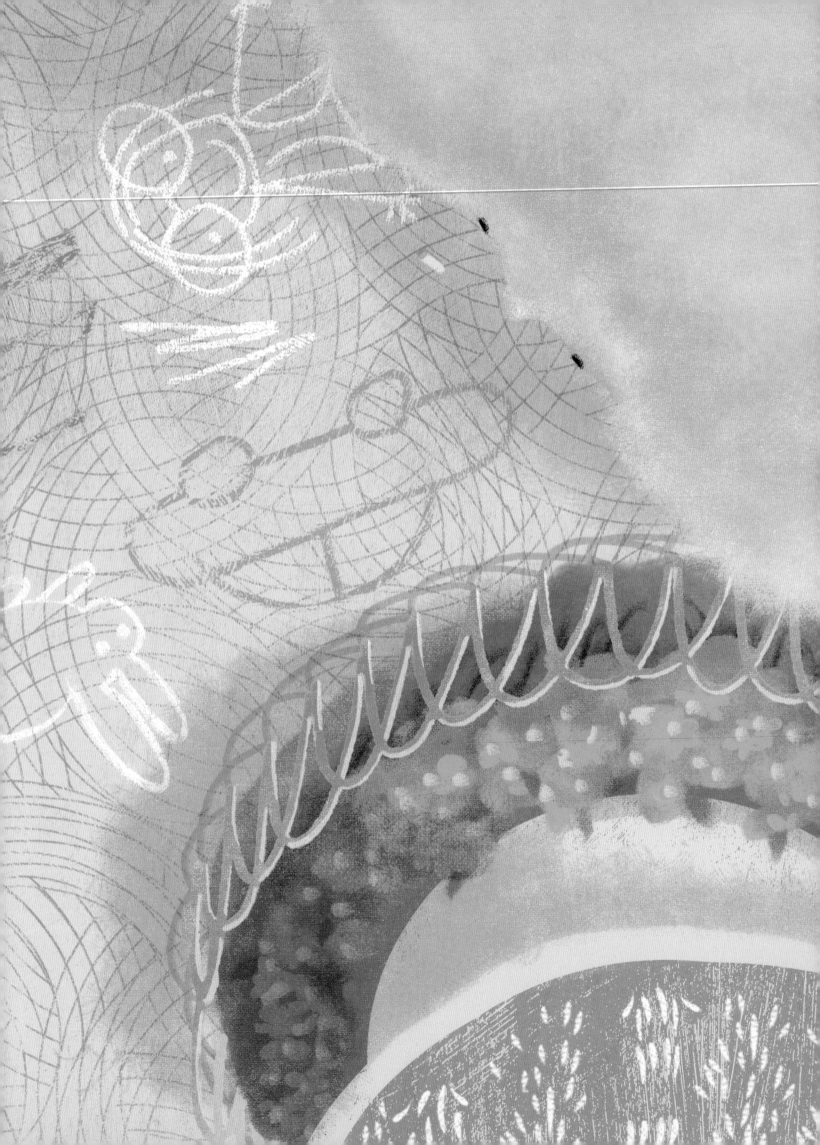

"Ooooh, I think it might be a love letter," said Mochi.

Kumo blushed happily and thought Mochi was probably right.

It had been a good day. A full day.

And now the day was done.

Kumo fell into a delicate, dreamy sleep.

A faint smile hanging in the air.

The day's light faded and the moon rose, full.
And in the sleepy sky, in the big changing sky,
the sunset clouds turned over, and their
backs were midnight blue.

In memory of my beautiful mother-in-law,
Naomi Ruth Binder Wall (1939–2020) — KM

Text copyright © 2022 by Kyo Maclear
Illustrations copyright © 2022 by Nathalie Dion

Library and Archives Canada Cataloguing in Publication

Title: Kumo: the bashful cloud / Kyo Maclear ; [illustrated by] Nathalie Dion.
Names: Maclear, Kyo, 1970- author. | Dion, Nathalie, 1964- illustrator.
Identifiers: Canadiana (print) 20210203994 | Canadiana (ebook) 2021020401X |
ISBN 9780735267282 (hardcover) | ISBN 9780735267299 (EPUB)
Classification: LCC PS8625.L435 K85 2022 | DDC jC813/.6—dc23

Published simultaneously in the United States of America by Tundra Books of Northern New York,
an imprint of Tundra Book Group, a division of Penguin Random House of Canada Limited

Library of Congress Control Number: 2021937900

Edited by Tara Walker with assistance from Margot Blankier
Designed by John Martz
The illustrations in this book are a mix of traditional and digital paintings, cut and transformed in Photoshop.
The text was set in Aesthet Nova.

Printed in China

www.penguinrandomhouse.ca

1 2 3 4 5   26 25 24 23 22

tundra | Penguin Random House
TUNDRA BOOKS

Glossary of Japanese words appearing in this book:

KUMO (koo-mo) = cloud
FUWA-CHAN (fu-wah-chan) = soft, fluffy and airy
MIRUKU (me-rue-koo) = transliteration of "milk"
MOCHI (mo-chee) = sticky rice cake